Little Ant
and the Dove

S.M.R. Saia

Illustrations by Tina Perko

One day, Little Ant ran into his great friend the stick insect. He was talking with some other insects, and they were comparing their abilities to avoid being eaten. Little Ant loved comparisons, especially when it turned out that he was better – or better at something – than anybody else. So Little Ant put down the seed that he was carrying and stopped to listen.

"I have the best way to trick birds," the ladybug said. "My bright colors warn birds that I will taste bad, so they don't want to eat me."

The housefly laughed. "I don't need to trick birds to stay safe," he said. "I am so fast that birds simply can't catch me."

Little Ant stepped closer and waited for a chance to tell them all that he, Little Ant, who was strong and smart, was also far too quick to be caught and eaten by a bird.

The weevil spoke up next. "I don't need to trick birds or outrun them. My armor is so strong that birds don't even think about eating me. Any bird that tries to have me for breakfast will chip his beak!" he said proudly.

Little Ant was impressed. He moved closer still and joined in as the others admired the weevil's strong armor.

"I'm sure you will all stay very safe," the stick insect said. "But I have to insist that when it comes to birds, no one is as safe as me. I blend in with the leaves and twigs on the ground. No bird even thinks to eat me, because no bird can see me."

The other insects all agreed that the stick insect was the best insect when it came to not being eaten.

"Come on, Little Ant," the stick insect said, as all the insects turned to go their separate ways. "I saw a black-eyed pea over there under that tree. Follow me, and I will take you to it."

So Little Ant left behind the rather tiny seed he had been carrying when he had come upon the group and started after the stick insect to get the black-eyed pea instead.

The weevil fell into step beside them. "Little Ant," the weevil said. "I saw some grains of wheat on the ground that I would like to take home, but I can't carry things as you can. Would you carry them for me, since you are going that way?"

"I'm sorry," Little Ant said. "I am going with my friend right now to find a black-eyed pea. I am too busy to do you a favor today."

"You could have helped the weevil," the stick insect said, as they left the weevil alone.

"Why should I?" Little Ant said. "What has the weevil ever done for me?"

"You never know when you might need the weevil to do you a favor," the stick insect told him as they came upon the weevil's grains.

"I doubt that," Little Ant said, smugly. After all, the weevil was not strong, or smart, or quick.

Soon, Little Ant could see the black-eyed pea. It was a monumental pea. A once-in-a-lifetime pea. He ran up to it and walked around the whole thing to inspect it. He hoisted it up onto his back and started off for home.

"Thank you," Little Ant said to his friend.

But before the stick insect could answer, a dove swooped down and grabbed him by one of his legs. "Help! Help!" the stick insect called as he sailed away. "Help me, Little Ant!"

Little Ant was so astonished that he dropped the black-eyed pea. The dove, with the stick insect dangling from her beak like a twig, flew up into the tree branches and landed in her nest.

Little Ant was in a panic. He had to do something! So he did the only thing that he could think to do. He scampered up the tree to the dove's nest. There, from a place of safety beneath a curl of bark, he saw his friend. The stick insect was still hanging from the dove's beak, wide-eyed and trembling.

"Mrs. Dove," Little Ant called in his biggest voice. "Please do not eat my friend."

The dove fixed a tiny black eye on Little Ant. "I am not going to eat anything," the dove said. "I am going to weave this twig into my nest."

"Please Mrs. Dove," Little Ant said. "Let my friend go, and perhaps someday I can do a favor for you."

"You are an insignificant little ant," the dove said. "I doubt that you will ever be in a position to do a favor for me." She tucked the stick insect's legs into the nest one at a time, snugly, so that he couldn't get loose. Then she flew away.

Little Ant stayed with his friend. The dove came and went, bringing back things to weave into her nest. She ignored Little Ant. The afternoon drug on. At one point, worn out from the fear and excitement, Little Ant dozed off. But he woke with a start when the dove landed suddenly in her nest, all a flutter, and cried, "Boys!"

A large stone sailed towards them and bounced off of the branch with a thunk. It was followed by another. A third stone hit the side of the nest and rattled it.

"Some boys followed me back across the field," the dove said. "They are hunting me. They are trying to kill me with their rocks! My eggs will be smashed!"

"Mrs. Dove," Little Ant said. "If I can make the boys go away, will you release my friend?"

"If you save my eggs, I will do anything," the dove said. Little Ant hurried down the side of the tree and across the ground to where the boys stood. In their hands, they each held more stones. Their pockets were heavy with them. There was no time to lose. Little Ant scampered up the side of one of the boys' shoes, halfway up his leg, and bit down hard.

"Ow!" the boy cried.
"Something is biting me!"

Little Ant hurried over to the
other boy and bit him, too.

"Ouch! Yow!" the second boy cried as Little Ant ran to safety. The boys dropped the rocks and ran off.

Little Ant called up to the dove, who had watched the whole thing. "Mrs. Dove, I saved your eggs. Will you please free my friend?"

"Gladly," the dove agreed. "One good turn deserves another!" She carefully unwove the stick insect from her nest, lifted him in her beak, and flew him down to the ground. Then she fluttered back up into the tree.

"Thank you," the stick insect said to Little Ant. "You saved my life!" Just then the weevil, who lived near the big tree, walked up.

"Weevil," Little Ant said. "I am sorry about this morning. I will go get some of my brother ants. Together, we will carry all of the wheat kernels back to your home for you."

"Thank you, Little Ant!" the weevil said.

A short time later, Little Ant and his brothers moved the wheat kernels for the weevil. The weevil walked along beside them, carefully rolling the black-eyed pea before him with his snout, so that the ants could take it back to their anthill when they were finished with their work. The stick insect, embarrassed about how he had boasted that morning, stayed close to his friends, checking the sky every so often for birds.

Published by Shelf Space Books
http://shelfspacebooks.com

ISBN: 978-1-945713-16-3